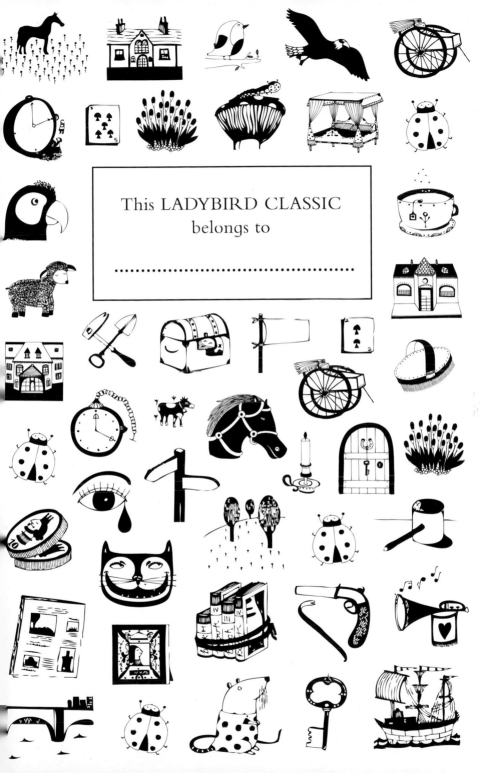

This LADYBIRD CLASSIC
belongs to

....

A History of the Author

Mary Shelley was born in London in 1797. She never had a formal education, but she made good use of her father's extensive library.

Shelley wrote several books, but her most famous was *Frankenstein*, published in 1818.

Chapter illustrations by Valeria Valenza

LADYBIRD BOOKS

UK | USA | Canada | Ireland | Australia

India | New Zealand | South Africa

Ladybird Books is part of the Penguin Random House group of companies whose addresses can be found at global.penguinrandomhouse.com.

Penguin
Random House
UK

First published 2015

002

Copyright © Ladybird Books Ltd, 2015

Printed in China

A CIP catalogue record for this book is available from the British Library

ISBN: 978–0–723–29706–2

LADYBIRD CLASSICS

FRANKENSTEIN

By Mary Shelley

Retold by Raymond Sibley
Illustrated by Monica Armino

Contents

CHAPTER ONE

FRANKENSTEIN

CAPTAIN WALTON AND his crew waited overnight for the thick ice around their ship to break. The morning brought relief, but as the men prepared to leave they saw a sledge drifting towards them on a large fragment of ice. There was a man aboard the sledge, nearly frozen and terribly emaciated.

The crew brought him on deck and

asked him why he had come so far upon the ice in such a strange vehicle.

'To seek one who fled from me,' the suffering man replied.

The tale which the man told next was a strange and terrifying one. It began years ago in his birthplace, Geneva.

Victor Frankenstein was his parents' first child and had a happy childhood filled with tenderness and love. The Frankensteins were good people, generous and kind to the poor.

At the age of five, when he was on holiday in Italy with his parents, Victor's mother called to him. Standing there with her was a beautiful, golden-haired little girl. She was about the same age as Victor. 'This is Elizabeth,' said his mother.

From the moment he saw her, Victor promised to always love and look after Elizabeth. His mother told him later that the girl was from a good family, but her

parents were dead. As she had no one to care for her, she was coming to live with them.

The two children grew up together. Elizabeth was calm and soft-voiced and, although Victor was a little short-tempered sometimes, they were happy, carefree and affectionate with one another.

When Victor was seven, his brother Ernest was born, and shortly afterwards the family moved for a while to their country house at Belrive. This second home was on the eastern shore of the lake, a short distance from the city gates of Geneva.

Apart from Elizabeth, Victor's only friend was Henry Clerval, the son of a merchant.

Victor felt there was something different inside him, but he told nobody about it – not even Elizabeth and Henry.

While Elizabeth loved the natural beauty of the Swiss countryside and Henry was excited by tales of knights in armour and stories of action and adventure, Victor's interest was in the darker side of nature. He thought deeply about the secrets and mysteries of life and death. These thoughts filled his mind so completely that he spent every minute he could alone, reading books on how life could be created and what happened to people's spirits after they had died.

Soon he turned to the study of ghosts and devils. A year or so later, his second brother, William, was born; by this time Victor had become completely fascinated by the subject.

One evening, when he was about fifteen, Victor saw something which had a great effect on him. A thunderstorm had formed over the Jura Mountains, and broke violently over the house and lake.

A flash of lightning shattered a tree close by the house. Victor never forgot the picture of the blasted stump and the power of electricity.

When Victor turned seventeen he was ready to begin his studies at the university of Ingolstadt, but tragically his mother died of scarlet fever.

On her deathbed she joined his hands with Elizabeth's. 'My children,' she said, 'it has always been my hope that one day you two will marry each other. Elizabeth, my love, be a mother to little William and Ernest.' She died calmly.

After a few weeks, Victor prepared to make the long and tiring coach journey to the university. He said goodbye sadly to his father, Elizabeth, his two young brothers and Henry Clerval.

'Please write to me often,' said Elizabeth tearfully.

CHAPTER TWO

THE DARK
EXPERIMENT

AFTER A FEW days at the university,
Victor Frankenstein decided that he would
spend his time exploring unknown powers
and the deep mystery of the creation of
life. He was so excited that he found it
difficult to sleep. It was all he thought
about. He was so deeply involved in his
experiments that, for the next two years,
he forgot about Elizabeth, his father, his

friend Henry and his brothers.

To begin with, he studied the medicine of life. He visited churchyards and burial chambers to observe the effect of death on the body. His mind always went back to the thunderstorm and the violent force of electricity. Could it create as well as destroy?

After many months' experimenting, he discovered how to harness that force to put life into something dead. He wondered how he should use the power he had gained. Victor decided to make a man!

He began his work in a lonely room at the top of his accommodation. He collected bodies from slaughterhouses, doctors' laboratories, churchyards and any place where the dead could be found.

It was a beautiful summer that year, but Victor did not notice; he could not tear himself away from what he was making in the upper room. Winter and spring followed, but he took no notice. He began to look

haggard; his nerves were on edge and he lost weight. But still Victor worked on.

One dreary November night he succeeded in giving a spark of life to his creation. By the light of a flickering candle he saw a limb twitch. The body breathed and one eye jerked open.

Victor Frankenstein looked down at the thing he had created. The skin was yellow and tightly stretched over the body. The creature was huge, but its eyes, under the dark hair, were watery. The flesh on the face was shrivelled and the lips were straight and blackish.

Now that he had succeeded, Frankenstein felt nothing but disgust. Once he had seen it, the horror became too much for him. He could not bear to look at the monster.

He rushed from the room in terror. Inside his own bedroom, he tried to calm himself. He lay on his bed fully clothed and fell into a fitful sleep. He had terrifying nightmares

of worms and his dead mother. Suddenly
he woke up. His forehead was damp with
sweat and his teeth chattered.

There at the foot of the bed stood the
creature, almost eight feet tall, its terrible
eyes staring at him. Its mouth opened as
it tried to speak. Victor leapt from the bed,
ran downstairs and hid in the courtyard,
petrified of meeting the demon corpse he
had given life to.

When it was light, the porter unlocked
the courtyard gates and Frankenstein
escaped into the streets of Ingolstadt.
He walked and walked, hoping that the
morning air would ease the heaviness
of his mind.

After some time, he found himself
outside the inn where the carriages
stopped. Something made him pause.
As he did, a familiar voice said, 'My dear
Victor, I'm so glad to see you. What a
lucky coincidence to find you walking

here just as I have arrived.'

It was Henry Clerval. Victor was delighted. 'You don't know how happy I am to see you, Henry, but what are you doing here?'

'I persuaded my father to let me come to the university to study with you.'

They talked of their families and friends.

'Your father, brothers and Elizabeth are all well and very happy, Victor, although they wish you would write to them more often,' said Henry. 'But you look ill and pale, as if you haven't slept for several nights.'

'Yes. You are right. I have been working hard on the same experiment for a long time and I have not had enough rest. That is finished now, I hope, so I promise to take more care,' said Victor.

Frankenstein led his friend in the direction of his college. He trembled inside at the idea that the creature might still be in his accommodation. The thought of seeing it again filled him with dread, but he feared even more that Henry might find out about it.

When they reached the bottom of the stairs Victor said, 'Please wait here for a moment, Henry.' Then he went up alone.

On the landing, he pulled himself together a little, but even so shivered with fright. He threw the door open and stepped in. The apartment was empty. The hideous monster had gone. Victor was so relieved that he ran downstairs to Henry.

'Let us have breakfast,' he cried. But Victor was so excited he could not sit still, laughing as he walked around the room.

Henry became worried. 'My dear Victor, what is the matter?'

'Nothing,' replied Victor. Then suddenly he imagined that the monster had crept back into the room, and he fainted from shock.

CHAPTER THREE

THE MONSTER'S FURY

AFTER HIS COLLAPSE, Victor remained in a lifeless state for several months, suffering from a nervous fever. During that time, his friend Henry nursed him and watched over him.

Not wanting Elizabeth or Victor's father to worry, Henry didn't let them know how ill Victor was. By spring, when the buds began to shoot on the trees outside his bedroom window, Victor was almost fully recovered. 'You are a good and kind friend, Henry. You've spent the whole winter nursing me. How shall I ever repay you?'

'First of all by writing to your father and Elizabeth. I have written many times, but it would put their minds at rest to have a letter in your handwriting.'

The months passed and the two friends spent the summer studying. The winter which followed was so severe that Victor's return home was delayed until May.

It was now almost three years since he had left Geneva. As he was preparing to depart, he received a letter from his father. The news it brought made him weep with bitterness and grief.

The letter told Victor that one evening his father had taken a walk with Elizabeth and Victor's two brothers. Little William had run on and hidden himself in the trees.

When his elder brother, Ernest, went to look for him, William was nowhere to be seen. As night came on, Elizabeth and Victor's father fetched torches from the house in Geneva so that they could carry on looking for the little boy. At about five o'clock in the morning, they found William's body. He had been killed. They could see bruises on his neck from the murderer's fingers.

Victor immediately took the coach home. He was comforted by the sight of the mountains and the lake near his home.

Later, as the night closed round him, he began to feel the grip of grief and fear. The city gates of Geneva were closed for the night, and Victor had to go to a village close by. He was unable to sleep, so he walked out to the place where William had been murdered. Before he reached it, a storm blew up and lightning soon flickered over the mountains and trees.

It was a beautiful sight. The thunder crashed over his head. In one flash of lightning, Victor saw a gigantic figure watching him. It was the monster!

In the next flash it was no longer there, but Frankenstein was now certain that the monster had killed little William. The thought sickened him.

He reached his home just after dawn, and Ernest met him. 'Father and Elizabeth are both ill with grief, Victor. Worse still, someone we all love has been arrested for the crime.'

Victor was stunned and unable to speak when he found out the accused person was Justine, a pretty, gentle girl who had lived with the Frankensteins for many years. She had nursed Victor's mother on her deathbed with great tenderness.

'Elizabeth says she will never believe it, whatever the evidence,' said Ernest.

'The poor girl is innocent,' agreed

Victor. 'She must be released.'

'Her trial is today, Victor,' replied Ernest, 'and it looks bad for her. She was ill on the morning the body was found, and stayed in bed for several days. During that time a servant found a locket in Justine's clothes. Elizabeth had given it to William on the day he disappeared.'

'She is innocent,' repeated Victor.

His father was overjoyed to see him again after such a long time, as was Elizabeth. She looked more beautiful than ever. Despite her grief, she showed Victor the greatest affection.

'Let us hope,' she said, 'that the judges do not convict Justine. If they do, I will never recover from it. We have lost darling William, but the innocent must not be punished for it.'

Once the trial started, Victor lived in torment. He could not speak out. Who would believe him? He had not seen the killing and, therefore, he could not produce the murderer.

Justine looked calm, but the onlookers took this to mean she lacked feeling and saw it as further proof of her guilt. Several witnesses were called. There were two main pieces of evidence against her: she had been seen near where the body was found, and William's locket containing a picture of his mother had been found in her clothes afterwards.

Justine told the court that on the night of the murder she had visited her aunt who lived in a village outside Geneva. When she returned at about nine o'clock, a man told her William was missing. She spent hours looking for him, by which time the city gates of Geneva were shut and she could not go home. She rested in a barn, sleeping on and off until dawn.

'I walked near the place of William's death by chance,' she pleaded, 'and I have no idea how I got the locket.'

Several people who could have spoken well of Justine did not come forward because they were frightened to be thought of as the friends of a murderess. Elizabeth had no such fears. She spoke for Justine in the crowded court, and told of the girl's fine character and of her gentleness and kindness. She reminded the listeners that Justine had nursed the late Madame Frankenstein with affection and care, and had loved little William as if he had been her own child.

'Justine would not have killed him for the picture,' said Elizabeth. 'She knows that we value her so much we would have given it to her.'

Although the people in the court were impressed by Elizabeth's generous appeal, it wasn't enough to convince them of Justine's innocence. When Victor saw the judges' faces, he rushed from the court in

anguish. He couldn't sleep that night.

Next morning, at the courthouse, Justine was found guilty. The following day she was executed.

CHAPTER FOUR

THE MONSTER MEETS HIS MAKER

VICTOR FELT THE pain of a tortured conscience. His unholy experiment had led to William and Justine losing their lives. He could not sleep, and his health was affected.

His father mistook Victor's guilt for intolerable grief. One day he said, 'You must not think only of William. We all loved him and are suffering, but it is our duty to think of the living.'

For a short time, Victor was strongly tempted to end his life. Then he thought of Elizabeth and his father and brother. How could he leave his dear ones unprotected against the creature?

In an attempt to forget, Victor went for a holiday in the nearby Alpine valleys. He covered the first part of the journey on horseback. Then, as the way became rugged and rough, he changed to a more sure-footed mule.

It was mid-August and he enjoyed the mountains, the rocks and the waterfalls. There was snow on the mountains and the glaciers almost reached the road. In the distance, he heard the rumbling of an avalanche. The higher he climbed, the more magnificent the sight was.

At last Victor felt at peace, and that night he slept soundly at a village inn. In the morning he felt so calm and happy in his surroundings that he decided to go higher. By noon he was looking down on a wide expanse of ice.

Suddenly he became aware of a huge thing, some distance away, running towards him at an astonishing speed. Victor began to tremble with rage, for as the shape approached he recognized the ugly creature he had brought into the world.

'You devil!' he shouted. 'How dare you come to me after what you have done! The tortures of hell are too mild for you!'

'I am so miserable,' replied the creature. 'I am hated and detested by all mankind. You made me, and yet you want to kill me. If you will do what I ask, I promise to leave you and your family in peace. If you refuse, I will destroy them all, one by one.'

But Victor was full of rage and he hurled himself at the monster, who easily held him off.

'Be calm. You must hear my story first,'

pleaded the monster. 'Have I not suffered enough? Remember that you made me bigger and stronger than you are, and I am your creature. I will be mild and gentle if you perform what I ask. There is goodness and happiness everywhere, but I am not allowed to share in it. You must make me happy, Frankenstein.'

'I will not. You are a wicked creature.'

'Please, Frankenstein. I am all alone. Everyone runs from me in disgust. The caves of ice and the wind and rain are kinder to me than mankind.'

'Cursed be the day I gave you life!'

'Frankenstein, believe me, I do not want to be wicked.'

'I do not want to be grief-stricken,' replied Victor. 'But you have made me so, you detestable fiend.'

'Listen to my story, Frankenstein,' said the creature, 'and then it will rest with you whether I live a gentle life or ruin you all.'

After a pause Victor said, 'Very well.
I will listen.'

They crossed the ice together and
entered a hut. The creature lit a fire and
then began its tale.

'When I ran away from your rooms in
Ingolstadt that night long ago, I was newly
made, and all my senses were confused.
I could not understand light or darkness or
heat, so I hid in the forest.'

'How did you stay alive?'

'I drank water from the brooks in the
forest and I ate berries from the trees. I was
cold and frightened in the dark and felt
helpless and miserable. In the daytime,
I liked to listen to all the forest sounds,
especially the songs of the birds.'

'Did anyone see you?'

'Not at first. I knew there were people
about because I found fire. Its warmth gave
me joy, but when I put my fingers into the
flame it hurt me. I found out that I could

eat nuts and roots as well as berries.'

'What made you leave the forest?'

'The search for food. I wandered for days. Soon the cold weather came on and it snowed. One day I saw a hut. The door was open, and I went in. An old man sat there. When he saw me, he screamed and rushed out of the hut, across the fields.'

The creature told Frankenstein that he had stayed in the warm hut and eaten some bread and cheese, and drank some milk and wine that had been left on the table.

'Afterwards, I walked to a small village. I wanted to be friendly, but the children shrieked in fear, and one woman fainted when she looked at me. The men threw stones at me until I ran away, bruised and frightened. Some distance away I found a disused hut, where I spent the night.'

In the morning he had noticed a cottage close by, but did not show himself as he

remembered how the villagers had treated him the day before. He decided to hide in the hut for as long as he could. It seemed like a palace to him.

In the cottage lived an old man and his son and daughter. The monster watched them through their window. They were unhappy, but affectionate with one another.

'For the first time, Frankenstein, I saw gentleness and kindness and love. When the girl took an instrument and played it, I heard music sweeter than birdsong. I was full of tears.'

Frankenstein looked at the creature. 'What is it you want me to do to make you happy?' he asked.

'Wait, Frankenstein. My story is not yet finished. The family were graceful and beautiful to look at and I wanted to join them, but I didn't dare to. Every day I listened to them and watched them. The old man was blind, and the two young ones

were miserable because they were very poor. Sometimes they gave their father food even when they had none for themselves.'

'Why then did you leave such good people?' asked Frankenstein.

'I did not want to, for I learned so much from them. The whole winter passed and neither Agatha, the girl, nor Felix, the boy, ever saw me.'

The monster explained that when they were unhappy he too was unhappy, and when they were full of joy, so was he. One day the creature saw his own reflection in a pool of water, and he turned away.

Often Felix gave some white flowers to his sister and the monster wanted to do the same, but he didn't dare to. Sometimes, though, during the nights, he would bring firewood and food for them. They were puzzled by this and wondered who had done it. The monster dreamed of the little family; to him they were superior beings.

Then one day an attractive young girl arrived on horseback. It seemed that her parents were dead and Felix and Agatha had befriended her in the past. Felix was in love with her and called her his 'sweet Arabian'. It soon became clear to the monster that the girl, whose name was Safie, was trying to learn more of her friends' language.

By listening to them talking together, the creature picked up more words, and when they were away he crept into their cottage to look at the books they used. He learned quickly, but the knowledge he gained made him sad.

'It made me realize, Frankenstein, that I was ignorant of my own creation and I had no friends, no relatives, no money and nothing of my own. All I had, apart from great strength and some intelligence, was a hideous face and an ugly shape. Where had I come from? I never had a father or mother. I had never been a child or had brothers or sisters. I had never been loved by anyone.'

Victor thought of his own happy childhood and looked at the monster for the first time with pity, but he did not speak.

'I had always been as I am, but until then I had known no evil.' The monster gave Frankenstein a terrible look before he spoke again.

'It disgusted me to think how I had been made. I have cursed you for it so many times I have lost count.'

The creature fell silent for a few moments. Then he told Victor how one day, when the father had been alone in the cottage, he had knocked on the door and entered. He had told the old man he was friendless and frightened, and that he would be an outcast forever. The blind man was sympathetic, and they had begun to talk easily together.

Then without warning the door had opened and Felix had come in with Safie and Agatha. Immediately Safie rushed out, Agatha fainted and Felix dragged his father away. As the creature tried to put its arms round the old man, Felix had beaten him off with a stick.

'I ran into the wood and stayed there until night,' the creature said. 'There was no one in the whole world who would pity me and no one who would help me. I spent the night in misery. A few days later I went back to the cottage but it was empty. I never saw any of them again.'

The creature looked sadly at Victor. 'My thoughts turned to you, Frankenstein, my creator. I knew you came from Geneva. The journey here was long and hard, and I travelled at night. Several times I lost my way. I wanted revenge.'

The creature's face softened a little. 'One day a little girl fell into a fast-flowing river near to where I was resting. I jumped into the water and dragged her to the bank.'

All of a sudden the monster leapt to his feet and shouted, 'A man aimed a gun at me and put a bullet in my shoulder! Then he lifted the girl and carried her away. The wound took a long while to heal and all the time I thought of how I had been treated. I swore to take revenge on all mankind.'

'But why,' exclaimed Victor, 'should you attack my innocent brother William?'

'It was not like that at all. I was resting one evening outside Geneva when a child came running near. The moment he saw me, he screamed and covered his eyes. I told him I would not hurt him, but he called me "wretch" and "ogre" and said he would tell his papa, Frankenstein the magistrate, to punish me.'

'And so you killed a little boy!'

'I did not intend to. He called me

dreadful names so I put my hands on his throat to silence him. In a moment he was dead.'

'An innocent girl has been executed for that!' shouted Victor.

'I took a locket from the boy's neck. It held a picture of a lady.'

'What did you do with it?'

'Something wicked. I found a barn to hide in, but a young woman was asleep on some straw. The fiend inside me told me to make her pay for the murder I had committed so I put the locket in her dress. After that, I wandered here. Now my story is finished.'

'When you began it,' said Victor, 'you said there was something I could do to make you happy.'

'Yes. I am alone and miserable. You must create another being: a woman as deformed and ugly as I am, who will live with me and love me and be my wife.

Only you can do it.'

'I refuse. Never again will I create a thing of wickedness.'

'You are wrong, Frankenstein,' replied the fiend. 'I want to live in peace with people, but they will not let me. If I cannot have love, I will cause fear.'

His face wrinkled in agony.

'Make a creature who loves me, who does not run from me, and I will make peace with you. Make me happy. Do not deny me! We will go away together and you will never see us again. I swear it. Please!'

Victor was upset by the creature's distress and, after a long pause, he said quietly, 'I consent. I will make you a mate.'

'Go then, Frankenstein, and begin your work.' The monster departed before Victor could reply or change his mind.

Victor sat for some time before making his way down towards the valley.

Darkness fell. At the halfway resting place, he sat down next to the fountain. He wept bitterly as he thought of what he had promised. By dawn, he had reached the village, and from there he went home to his family.

Victor feared the monster's fury, but, as much as he tried, he could not bring himself to start work on another creation. His mind was also taken up with Elizabeth, who had accepted his proposal of marriage.

'I am so happy, Victor,' said his father. 'When will the wedding be?'

Victor did not reply immediately. The thought of marrying Elizabeth while the monster still threatened him filled him with horror. He knew that he would have to give the monster a mate first, and he could not set up a laboratory in the house in case it was discovered. His father had tried to persuade him many times to take a long holiday to restore his health completely, and now he agreed.

It was decided that Victor should go to England for at least six months, then marry Elizabeth upon his return to Geneva. Henry Clerval was to accompany him.

Although it worried Victor that he was leaving his family and future bride open to attack from the monster, he remembered that the creature had said he would follow Frankenstein wherever he went.

CHAPTER FIVE

FRANKENSTEIN'S NEW CREATION

IN SEPTEMBER, VICTOR packed as many of his chemical instruments as he could. Then he and Henry made their way by coach across Europe. From Rotterdam they crossed the sea by ship to Dover.

In England, Victor began to collect the materials necessary for his new creation. The weeks passed, then they received an invitation to visit Scotland. Victor made an excuse not to go so he could continue with his work. He went to a desolate and remote island off the Scottish coast and tried to begin. There were just five other people on the island.

The task sickened him and he grew restless and nervous, dreading that the monster might appear.

What if this female became more violent than her mate? What if she and the creature disliked one another? What if she did not agree to go away and leave Frankenstein? What if his creations had children together who themselves were monsters? All these questions weighed on his mind.

One evening as he worked, he looked up and saw the monster watching him through the window, a dreadful smile on his face. All of a sudden, Frankenstein realized what he was doing and in a fit

of passion he tore the thing he had been making to pieces.

Outside the window the monster howled. 'After I have waited so long, you have destroyed what you promised me. You are my creator, Frankenstein, but I am your master now. I will have my revenge. Remember me, Frankenstein, because I shall be with you on your wedding night!'

After he had gone, Victor's mind was in a whirl. The monster's words kept swirling around in his head. '*I shall be with you on your wedding night.*' The night passed. Frankenstein could not sleep.

In the morning, a fisherman brought Victor some letters. One was from Henry Clerval, who suggested that Victor should join him. He decided to go.

First, however, he went into his laboratory and put the remains of the half-finished creature into a large basket.

Just after midnight, he took a small boat and, when he was about four miles from shore, dropped the basket, which he had weighted with heavy stones, into the sea.

Two days later, he reached the town where Henry was staying and made his way to his friend's accommodation. He was too late! The fiend had got there before him. Henry was dead, with the mark of the monster's fingers on his neck. Victor looked at the lifeless form of his friend; he shook violently and collapsed in a fever.

When Victor was found beside the body, he was suspected of being the murderer. He was arrested and a trial was arranged. For two months, Victor stayed in his prison cell, raving like a madman. The magistrate tried to question him, without success.

As he regained his health, Victor thought often of Justine, executed in innocence. Maybe he would suffer the same penalty. Then one day the magistrate returned.

'When you first became ill,' he explained, 'I examined the papers from your pocket and was able to trace your family. We know now that you were a close friend of Mr Clerval and the shock of his murder made you ill again. Your father has arrived here to take you home.'

When he saw his father, the first words Victor said were, 'Are Elizabeth and Ernest well protected?'

His father assured him they were safe.

The court dismissed the case against Victor and he left prison with his father. On the way home, his father tried to make Victor more cheerful by talking about the forthcoming marriage to Elizabeth. All Victor could think of was watching over his loved ones until he could destroy the monster forever.

CHAPTER SIX

FINAL REVENGE

ON THE JOURNEY home, Victor told
his father that he had been the cause of
the deaths of William, Justine and Henry,
but his father would not hear of it.

'My dear son, please don't say that
again,' he said softly.

So Victor remained silent, but the
words of the monster came back to him.
'*I shall be with you on your wedding night.*'

He was convinced that on that night the creature would try to kill him.

Elizabeth's eyes filled with tears when she saw how thin and frail Victor was. She was as sweet and gentle as she had always been. Victor wanted desperately to marry her. In the meantime, while preparations went ahead for the wedding, he made sure he always had loaded pistols and a dagger within reach.

It was decided that the couple should spend their honeymoon at a villa beside the lake where Elizabeth's parents had lived. After the ceremony, the newlyweds left by boat from Geneva, planning to stay that night at Evian. They landed at eight in the evening. Before returning to the inn, they walked along the lake's shore, but the words of the monster would not stay out of Victor's mind. '*I shall be with you on your wedding night.*'

He was so agitated that, when

Elizabeth went to their room, he felt he had to find out where the monster was. As he was walking up and down the passages of the house, he heard dreadful screams from Elizabeth.

Victor rushed into their room, but he was too late. His bride was lying across the bed, lifeless, with the mark of the fiend's grasp on her neck. Looking through the bare window was the hideous murderer. He pointed his finger at the body of Elizabeth, and laughed.

Frankenstein ran to the window and fired his pistol, but the creature moved with the swiftness of light and plunged into the lake. The noise of the pistol shot brought a crowd into the room. When Victor pointed to the lake, they took to the boats and followed the murderer, but it was all in vain. After several hours they returned.

Frankenstein collapsed from

exhaustion and was put to bed. The full horror of all that had happened grew in his mind. The killing of William, the execution of Justine, the murder of Henry, and now his own wife. The idea that his father and his brother Ernest were in danger made Victor shudder. He decided that he must act.

He returned to Geneva. The news of what had happened broke Victor's father. He had loved Elizabeth as his own child. A few days later, he died in Victor's arms.

In his despair, Victor formed a plan to pursue his monster until he could destroy it. Before leaving Geneva he paid his last visit to the cemetery where the bodies of William, Elizabeth and his father rested. It was getting dark as he knelt on the grass and prayed aloud for help to find and kill the cursed monster.

As if in answer, out of the stillness came a loud and wicked laugh. Then the

creature said softly, 'I am satisfied, Frankenstein, now that you are miserable and wretched.'

With that, he took off at great speed.

For months Victor trailed the monster, guided by small clues, but he could never catch up with him. He traced the monster along the windings of the river shore, and followed him closely along parts of the Mediterranean coastline.

Through country after country the monster kept a day ahead of Victor, then by ship across the Black Sea, then amidst the wilds of Tartary and the wastes of Russia. All the time the creature avoided populated places.

Each time Victor lost trace of him, the fiend would return and leave some mark. He was enjoying tormenting Victor, who had no peace except when he was asleep. But by day, the thought of revenge kept him going.

One night Victor heard a voice in the darkness: 'You must follow me now to the bitter cold and ice of the north. There you will have more hard and miserable hours to endure before I am satisfied that you have suffered enough, my enemy.'

On Victor went. Then, when the cold was almost too severe to bear, he saw a speck in the distance. Just when it seemed he had caught up with his enemy, the wind rose, the sea roared, and the ice cracked and split. He was left drifting on a shattered piece of ice.

His mind was filled with thoughts of William, Justine, Henry, Elizabeth and his father. He thought of his own life and how he had thrown his talents aside. His strength ebbed away. Victor was now totally exhausted.

This is how Captain Walton and his men came across Frankenstein and learned of his terrible tale. Some time

after, Victor finally closed his eyes.

Realizing he was no longer being tracked, the monster returned to look for his maker. When he saw Victor's body in the cabin, he was overcome with grief and horror.

'Forgive me, Frankenstein. I destroyed everything you loved. But I have suffered great hardships myself. You cannot hear me say this, but I did not want to kill them. Anyway, it is all ended now. You are my last victim.'

The creature bowed his head in misery. 'Why did Felix drive me from the cottage? Why did the peasant shoot me when I saved his child? Is that why I have murdered the lovely and the helpless? Now you are dead, Frankenstein. What is there left for me, but death?'

The monster turned and disappeared into the darkness.

Collect more fantastic
LADYBIRD 🐞 CLASSICS

Alice in Wonderland
9781409311232

Oliver Twist
9781409311256

Treasure Island
9781409311287

BLACK BEAUTY
9781409311249

GULLIVER'S Travels
9781409311270

The Secret Garden
9781409311263

A Christmas Carol
9781409312215

Peter Pan
9781409312222

The Three Musketeers
9781409313557

THE WIND IN THE WILLOWS
9781409313564

Heidi
9781409313571

The Jungle Book
9781409313588

Little Women
9780723270874

The Railway Children
9780723270867

Robin Hood
9780723295594

KING ARTHUR
9780723295600

Dracula
9780723297055